A BITE OF MURDER

THE DEAD-END DRIVE-IN SERIES, BOOK 5

CAROLYN Q. HUNTER

SUMMER PRESCOTT BOOKS PUBLISHING

Copyright 2018 Summer Prescott Books

All Rights Reserved. *No part of this publication nor any of the information herein may be quoted from, nor reproduced, in any form, including but not limited to: printing, scanning, photocopying or any other printed, digital, or audio formats, without prior express written consent of the copyright holder.*

**This book is a work of fiction. Any similarities to persons, living or dead, places of business, or situations past or present, is completely unintentional.

PROLOGUE

Jason's lungs burned with the wet night air. Each breath in and out felt like pins and needles in his chest and a fire in his throat. With the beating of his heart, blood ran up into his head sending pounding waves of pain behind his eyes.

To add insult to injury, his legs felt like two leaden logs. He could barely feel them, and the joints assumed a consistency that felt like gelatin. He was ready to fall over and pass out at any second, his vision blurring as he wheezed.

How long had he been running? How long since he'd been forced off the road by that renegade truck?

He'd been on his way home from the real estate office in downtown Sunken Grove. The rural bayou roads were always a little dark at this time of night, but Jason had kept his wits about himself as he navigated his way back to his house.

He was used to the occasional alligator sitting up on the pavement and having to go around it, but he hadn't planned for the high beams of a random pickup truck to come barreling toward him at top speed down the wrong side of the road.

He'd been forced to jerk the wheel at the last second to avoid a collision with the other vehicle. Unfortunately, this action created an issue as his two front tires sunk in the muck of the bayou. There would be no getting it out without calling for a tow truck.

The person who'd so recklessly come at him had stopped their truck and climbed out. At first, Jason had been positive that whoever it was behind that wheel had been drinking. What other reason could there be for such mindless behavior?

However, once he realized the person getting out of the truck was wearing a makeshift mask made from burlap and was carrying some sort of knife, he didn't hesitate to question the situation. Clearly, whoever this was intended to hurt him.

That was when he'd run out into the dark bayou.

Stopping for a second, he leaned down with his hands on his knees and drew in a heavy breath. It felt like he'd been running for nearly an hour.

Looking over his shoulder through the rows of cypress trees on the bayou, he couldn't spot his pursuer. Had he finally managed to lose the maniac? He hoped that he had, leaning his back against a tree and taking large gulps of air.

Standing still, the faint sound of music played out along a fresh breeze. It had a cinematic and orchestral style to it, Jason could tell that much. However, where was it coming from?

Then he remembered. The drive-in theater was out this direction.

"That's it," he whispered, pushing off from the tree and picking up his pace again. Following the noise, he hoped that he could reach the drive-in—and subsequently, the crowds of moviegoers—before the maniac figured out where he was.

Jason knew he would be safe once he was in sight of other people. He could use the theater's phone to call the police and have them send out some officers to apprehend the person who had chased him off the road.

"Come on, come on," he begged, hearing the music swell louder in a dramatic movement.

He had to be getting close. Finally, the bluish quality of light he knew had to be coming from the projector passed through the trees. Bursting into a run, he jumped out from between a low brush and nearly ran into a tall wooden wall. He instantly realized he was standing behind the drive-in's screen.

A hissing noise and a woman screaming accompanied the music beyond coming from the many cars that had tuned into the radio station that played the audio for the film. Jason had been to the theater only once but knew their set-up.

He was grateful that some of the patrons had hefty car sound systems to reach him out in the bayou.

Still, he wasn't out of the woods yet. To get to the main building and connected restaurant, he'd have to walk all the way around the fence. "Okay, I can do this," he told himself. Spinning around, he was about to head to the nearest corner of the fence and make an all-out sprint for the entrance.

However, instead of running, he stopped—impaling himself on the killer's outstretched blade. He screamed out in desperation as he realized he was dying, but his own voice was drowned by the screams of the woman in the film.

Jason fell down dead on the wet ground.

CHAPTER ONE

The piercing sound of screams jolted though Anna-Lee Francis' ears, causing her to cringe as she took the window service tray off one of the cars who had finished their meal. She lifted her head and looked at the film screen with a somewhat confused expression marring her brow.

Dracula Has Come from the Crypt was just nearing its climax. The titular character and the young college student hero were wrestling at the edge of a balcony overlooking a cliff. In the background near the old castle door, a platinum blonde and busty woman screamed like a maniac, her fingers clutching the sides of her face in a rather melodramatic performance.

Within the next second, Dracula fell over the edge

and landed directly on top of a pointed gold cross. A spurt of blood that looked an almost neon shade of red, and very fake, erupted from his chest as he was impaled.

The actor let out a cry, wiggling around like a maniac with his hands in the air before going limp and letting out a long dramatic breath.

Anna rolled her eyes as she carried the tray back toward the restaurant, thinking the scream she'd heard that had seemed so real was probably just a trick of sound waves bouncing in between cars. The Voodoo Drive-In was Anna's younger sister's business, as well as her beloved baby.

Sarah-Belle had a sick fascination with the macabre and especially enjoyed older horror flicks. The drive-in was known for showing these types of films, movies that Anna probably would never consciously choose to sit down and watch if she didn't work as an assistant manager at her sister's business.

Anna had to admit, however, that these nineteen-sixties British monster movies were the absolute worst. The black and white films at least had some class, but the colorized versions of Dracula, Frankenstein, The Mummy, and all the rest of the traditional spooks were so goofy she had a hard time stomaching them. They were all made by the same company called *Anvil* that had long gone out of business.

While Belle had argued that the films were purposefully made to be over the top, Anna just couldn't be talked into liking them.

Unfortunately, at the moment, the theater was doing a two-week Dracula marathon. Each night they showed another one of the *Anvil* vampire films. It was only the third night of the event and Anna was ready to tear her hair out. She'd seen enough dripping fangs, red eyes, and screaming women to last a million years in her estimation.

Reaching the service window at the back of the two-story brick building, she handed the tray through to Valerie Bronson, the other manager at the drive-in. "How many more trays are out in the parking lot?" Valerie asked, making sure the hair net was straight over her black dreadlocks.

Valerie, along with her husband Chief Dan Bronson, was like a parental figure to the "Drive-In Sisters" as they were quickly becoming known as. Anna and Belle had lost their biological parents a while back and the chief of police of the small Louisiana town and his wife had swooped in to act as caretakers and emotional support where they could.

"Three more, I think. Most everyone else finished their food before the halfway mark."

"Okay, let's just make sure no one steals them this time. We've lost two trays this last month to teenagers who just didn't feel like waiting for us to collect the tray."

Anna rolled her eyes. "Why would you want to steal a window tray? What are they going to use it for?"

Valerie clicked her tongue distastefully. "Nothin. They just like the thrill of taking it. Dan thinks he'll figure out exactly which kids took em, but I'm not holding my breath."

"Well, it has been quiet here lately. No more ghosts or murders," she said.

"No ghosts? What about me?" came a complaint from inside the kitchen.

Anna tried not to pay attention to the Drive-In's resident ghost—a voodoo practitioner who'd found himself trapped inside the black and white character of Frederick Loren from the movie House on Haunted Hill. Some mumbo jumbo magic had gotten its supernatural wires crossed and now they had a walking talking ghost that only the sisters could see who looked exactly like Vincent Price.

While both Valerie and Dan believed and practiced voodoo themselves, and therefore weren't ones to overlook the possibility of supernatural occurrences, the sisters had not told them about their friendly ghost.

They did, however, know about the potential ghostly involvement in some murder cases that had happened over the past year or so. Dan had grumbled about not being able to put the full story into his police report. What state officials, or other officers for that matter, would believe that spooks were involved in the occasional crime?

In Sunken Grove, however, the population was no stranger to the paranormal. While there were many who were unbelievers, the fact of the matter was the small town seemed to attract all sorts of strange and unexplainable occurrences.

Anna, who hated the paranormal on any level, tried to avoid ghosts like the plague.

Her only exception was Harlem, or Vincent if you wanted to be funny. Harlem was his real name from when he was alive. In the past months, this transparent and otherworldly being had become one of Anna's best friends and confidants.

Harlem stuck his nose up in the air and huffed. "I'm offended."

Anna rolled her eyes, walking to the edge of the service window and stepping in the back door of the restaurant. "How is Belle?" she asked, knowing her sister was in bed in the upstairs apartment on the second floor.

"Still as sick as a dog," Valerie sighed. "I don't know if it's a cold, spring allergies, or something else."

"Probably both," Anna admitted, washing her hands in the sink to get a ketchup stain off. Some customers weren't as clean as others when it came to the food trays. "You know how she is. It's like a tradition. She always gets a cold in the spring, never in the fall or winter."

"I know, but she seems worse this time around," Valerie admitted, sorting through some of the receipts and getting a start on the nightly book work.

Anna only shrugged. "Can you hold down the fort for a second? I'm going to check on her."

"Will do. Make sure she is getting lots of fluid," she said in a motherly fashion.

"I know." Anna stepped out into the dining room of the restaurant—which was only open each night until the movie started—and headed up the brick staircase behind the bar. Walking through the apartment, she found her sister on the couch then looked out through a window toward the movie screen.

"Hey, why aren't you sleeping?" she scolded her younger sister.

"I couldn't. Besides, I didn't want to miss the movie," Belle complained through a nasal voice.

Anna sat on the arm of the couch. "You can watch this movie whenever you want. The theater owns a million different films."

Belle made a snorting sound, a result of just trying to breathe normally. "I know that, but I wanted to see it."

Anna couldn't help but smile. In the past year, she'd been forced to rely on Belle after making an emergency move back to Sunken Grove. Things hadn't gone according to plan and Anna had gone broke. She leaned on Belle's good charity—and the success of the drive-in—to get her through. She was glad for a job, even if it was under Belle.

At this moment, however, with Belle sick and unable to do her normal work on the place, Anna was having flashbacks to when they were younger. Especially after their parents passed away, Anna had spent many a spring night sitting with Belle through a cold. It felt nice to be needed in that way again.

"Well, are you at least drinking water?"

"I've had to pee like a thousand times tonight."

"I'll take that as a yes," she said with a smirk. Anna looked out the window and saw that the credits were rolling. Cars were getting ready to pull out. "I better get back down there and collect the last few trays before everyone runs off."

"Good idea," Belle agreed. "Do you mind picking up the trash near the screen tonight? The wind has been blowing and whatever people decide to just toss out gets carried up there in a pile."

Anna didn't like the idea of standing outside in the

muggy air to pick up garbage, but if Belle wanted it, she would comply. "Okay. I'll pick it up, but I can't guarantee I'll do a thorough job tonight."

"I understand."

"I just don't see why people can't take care of their own trash."

"Eh, they get lazy, is all. It's never that much trash."

"I hope so," Anna said, patting her sister on the head before heading back downstairs.

CHAPTER TWO

She hurried out to the lot and collected up the remaining trays, just catching the last one before a car full of teenage girls all drove off back to their homes. She wanted to scold them but refrained.

Once the trays were all washed and put away and the parking lot was empty, Anna took the trash grabber and a plastic bag. "I sure hope there isn't a ton of junk out here," she complained as she made her way across the lot, realizing that Harlem was floating next to her. "Why don't *you* pick it up?" she asked him in a joking manner.

"Believe me, even if I could . . . I wouldn't," he said, chuckling to himself.

"Typical," she groaned.

"Naw. In reality, when I was alive I did all my own cleaning and chores. I had to keep a tidy store and a clean house. I could never stand clutter."

"But you ran a voodoo shop. Those are *always* cluttered," Anna pointed out, thinking of their very own voodoo shop in the downtown area that tourists liked to call *The Little French Quarter*. Payton Shaw who owned it was as absent-minded and disorganized as they came. His shop always looked a mess.

"Well, to appease the masses you sort of have to keep a certain atmosphere in a store like that. They want to see skulls, candles, and trinkets all stacked up together in a dusty mess."

Anna nodded, reaching the screen and letting out a breath of relief to see only a few napkins and cups had found their way over. "I can see what you mean," she said, responding to Harlem and pinching the first piece of garbage with the grabbers. She lifted it into the bag. "Did you ever spread dust on things?"

Harlem floated nearby, letting out a low laugh. "As a matter-of-fact, yes. I did do that once or twice."

Anna couldn't help laughing out loud. "That's

ridiculous," she said. As she went about picking up more trash, she couldn't help but wonder if bringing up his past life was hard for him. Did he miss being alive? What was it really like to be dead?

She didn't know, and she didn't want to ask, although knowing that there *was* something after death, even if it was just a life of a ghost haunting a drive-in, was strangely comforting.

"So, what did you think of the movie tonight?" he asked, breaking into her thoughts.

"Oh, I don't know. It was just way too goofy for my tastes. I can't believe that I have to sit through another week and a half of this."

"Ah, it isn't so bad. I think they're sort of fun," he admitted.

"Says the man who is from a goofy horror flick."

"A black and white horror flick, remember?" he pointed out.

Looking at his flickering black and white body, she shook her head. "How could I forget?" She pinched a cup lid in between the grabber's fingers. "You know, that last scene had some weird sound going on. I could have sworn I actually heard someone screaming, but then I realized it was just the movie."

"What if it wasn't?" Harlem teased, waving his fingers in the air. Seeing a ghost do the traditional little wave was a bit funny.

"What else could it be? A girl screaming at her boyfriend to stop trying to kiss her during the movie?"

Harlem wiggled his eyebrows. "Maybe someone was murdered . . . right behind the movie screen," he announced, waving his arm in a dramatic motion that mimicked the evening's movie.

Anna couldn't help laughing again. Harlem used to scare her, but now he made her laugh a lot. Although, sometimes he liked jumping out of walls or through doors to scare her. She didn't care for that. He even came down to her apartment in town on occasion unannounced. He could be a nuisance when he wanted to be.

"I doubt anyone was murdered. I think people would have noticed someone *actually* screaming."

"You never knoooooow," he said, dragging out the O

in a traditional ghostly sound as he floated back through the screen.

Anna picked up the last piece of trash in site and deposited it in the bag. "Have fun looking for dead bodies. I'm heading back," she announced.

Harlem's head appeared through the screen, giving her a brief jump.

"Oh, stop doing that all the time."

He frowned. "Uhm. I think you should see this."

"See what?" she demanded, wanting to get back to the building so she could finish up her closing duties and head home. She was just glad she didn't have to input the day's numbers like Valerie was doing. Usually, Belle did that part of it, but Val wouldn't allow her to do a single thing while she was sick.

"I . . ." he hesitated, "I think there really is a dead body back here.

Anna laughed, waving the ghost off. "You and your jokes. Now stop playing around and come inside with me. Otherwise, just hang out here."

"I'm not joking," he said flatly, a hint of urgency coming into his voice.

Looking at him again, she saw the serious expression that had encompassed his black and white face.

"You're joking. Please tell me you're joking," she pleaded. The last thing she needed, the drive-in needed, was another dead body on their hands. She, Harlem, and Belle had dealt with a few strange murders.

"I'm not joking," he insisted.

"You've gotta be kidding me." Rushing to the side of the screen, she peered through a loose board in the fence. Surely enough, there was a man lying face down in the mud, a puddle of blood oozing around him. It appeared he'd been shot or stabbed. "No. No way," she spat out.

"You better give Dan a call," Harlem said.

CHAPTER THREE

"A body? You've got to be kidding me," Belle exclaimed, sitting bolt upright. The instant she did, she let out a woozy sigh and let herself fall back onto the couch.

"I knew we shouldn't have told her," Anna scolded Harlem who was looking out the window at the flashing lights of the police car in the lot below. The chief and his singular officer were cordoning off the scene, preparing to do some investigating.

Anna had told Valerie what was happening and called Dan before even mentioning a dead body to her sister. However, Harlem said they should tell her right away. After all, she was going to see the flashing lights.

"Who is it?"

"We don't know," Anna put her hands up in the air. "We're going to keep our hands clean of it this time. No investigating on our part," she insisted.

Belle scowled at this reaction to the body. "How can you say that? We've helped Dan solve a few cases now."

"And that doesn't make us police officers."

"More like private eyes," Harlem thought out loud, folding his arms.

Anna turned and gave him a death glare. "No. Not like private eyes. We are two sisters who run a drive-in theater."

Belle sat up again, slower this time. "Come on. What police officer has a partner who can go into crime scenes and suspects houses without being detected whatsoever?" she pressed, pointing at their ghostly friend.

Anna pursed her lips, trying not to swear at her sister. "We're not getting involved," she reiterated.

"And why the heck not?" she demanded.

"First of all, you're sick. Second, we aren't crime professionals. Third, why should we?" she insisted.

"Okay, first, I'll be better tomorrow," Belle retorted.

"No, you won't."

"Second," she continued without a beat, "we aren't crime professionals, but we do have more of an understanding of the paranormal aspects in these cases."

"There is nothing paranormal going on here," Anna shot back.

"Third, why should we? Because the body was found at our drive-in."

"It's outside the drive-in," the older sister argued, trying her best to keep Belle at bay. Anna knew she had a protective side—and it had come out tenfold with her sister being sick—but she especially wanted to keep Belle away from any murderers.

"Close enough. I mean, how does that reflect on our business?" she asked.

"Quite well, actually," Harlem chimed in. "This place is reportedly haunted, which it is," he said, motioning to himself with both hands. "Each time there is a weirdo paranormal occurrence or murder here, our customer numbers skyrocket. You know that best of all," he said to Belle who usually balanced the books.

Belle rolled her eyes. "I was trying to convince my sister here that we should help investigate. You're not helping, Harlem."

"The point is, tourists are starting to come in from all over to see our movies. Most of them are true crime and paranormal fanatics. They eat this kind of stuff up. Not to mention, New Orleans is already a target for those types and we're just a hop, skip and a jump over to Cajun Country," he said.

"Anyway, we're not investigating. That's that," Anna said, waving her hands across in front of her.

Belle grumbled but leaned back into the couch.

A quiet knock came on the door and Anna walked over to answer it. A chubby dark-skinned man with a bald head and bushy mustache stepped inside. "Hi, girls."

"Any news, Dan? Who is it?" Belle asked, sitting up again, but then having to bob back down.

Anna sighed, knowing her sister needed rest and relaxation and this new murder was going to make that impossible.

"I'm afraid to say it's one of our own from town."

"Who?" Anna gasped, now just as interested as her sister in the case.

"Jason Dobbs, I'm afraid."

Belle gasped, putting a hand up to her mouth.

"Jason?" Anna asked, not recognizing the name. Having lived away from Sunken Grove for a couple years, she didn't know or remember everyone from around town.

"Yep. He's a realtor and landlord for a lot of property in town."

Belle removed her hand from her mouth. "He's the man who sold me this property to set up the drive-in. I can't believe it. He seemed so nice."

"Who would want to kill him?" Anna asked, unable to stop the curious questions from spilling out. She felt ashamed, knowing how she had just as much a nose for crime as her sister. She just had the logical sense to stay out of it when she could.

"I don't know, but there wasn't a murder weapon on the scene. We'll have to do a full search of the grounds and surrounding bayou for it."

"What about in the restaurant?" Belle asked.

"I doubt it's in here, but if we deem it necessary, we'll take a peek."

"I'll help," Belle insisted.

"No, you won't," Anna ordered, pushing her back onto the couch.

"She's right, this is police work. I'll let you know if we find anything." With that, he headed back down the stairs.

"What if the killer left it somewhere here in the restaurant?" Belle said.

"How would they do that?" Anna demanded.

"I don't know. I have to look," she said, going to sit up again.

"No, you don't," Anna said. "If it makes you feel better, I'll have a quick look around the restaurant myself." Somehow, she felt like she was going to regret this.

CHAPTER FOUR

Being left alone again on the couch, Belle quickly drifted off to sleep, not realizing just how worn out she was. In her dreams, she had images of murder victims and ghosts . . . all while she was trapped inside and unable to do anything.

When her eyes fluttered open again, it appeared to be light outside. She'd slept all the way through the night without a single inkling as to what had happened with the body, the police, or the murder weapon. Belle let out a long rush of air, buzzing her lips as she did. Her head still felt heavy, as if it were full of water. It had the sensation of sloshing around and making her dizzy. It was accompanied by a dull headache that just sort of throbbed in the background behind her eyes. Her vision felt fuzzy, like fingers reaching inside her skull. To make matters worse, she could hardly draw in a good breath without having to work at it.

She hated being sick like this and hated it worse now that there seemed to be so much going on around the drive-in. It had been enough that she had to step down from her usual work duties because of this blasted cold, but it was ten times worse now knowing that there was a murder investigation going on right on her property and she couldn't do a single thing about it.

Unfortunately, when it came to being sick, you didn't get much of a choice.

She'd practically fallen over working on a batch of Cajun fries in the kitchen the afternoon before. Thankfully, Valerie had been there to catch her. She and Anna dragged her up to bed and ordered her to stay put until she was well again. "You should have said you weren't feeling well," Valerie had scolded her.

Belle, being the spitfire that she was, hadn't thought she'd had the option to bow out of work. The drive-in was her baby, and she hated leaving it in the hands of Valerie and Anna alone. It wasn't that she didn't trust them, she did, but the drive-in was her own responsibility and she liked to be there when things were happening.

Having the vampire marathon scheduled this month had been a poor choice, she realized. It was a large undertaking and she always did tend to get ill around this time of year. The restaurant downstairs had been decked out in foam stone pillars and archways that she'd crafted herself using materials she'd saved from packages she'd gotten in the mail. The tables were draped with red cloths with gold trim. Plastic and rubber bats hung from the ceiling and all red and black drinks from the bar—Bloody Mary's, Blackberry Margaritas, Grim Reapers, Soul Takers—were on a special.

It had been a big ordeal to get set up, and Belle had been proud of herself. The patrons loved it as well, especially the adults who were enjoying the beverages.

Yet, she had still managed to get sick right at the beginning of it all.

She couldn't plan her life around the chance of getting sick, could she?

Not to mention, now that a huge thing like a murder had come up, she was feeling antsy, like she couldn't lay still despite the achiness in all of her muscles.

Groaning through her sore throat, Belle gripped the back of the couch and slowly lifted herself up. Her head swam for a second, but she managed to squeeze her eyes tight until the sensation passed. While everyone else was out trying to figure out this latest mystery, she was stuck up her like a princess locked in a tower.

However, maybe she didn't need to be.

She decided that she wasn't feeling quite as poorly as the evening before. Maybe she could try getting up and doing a few things before Valerie and Anna came back to the drive-in that morning.

Placing her feet on the cold hardwood floor, she took a second to compose herself before standing up. It was a wobbly process, but she managed it. A woman with determination, she shuffled over to the bathroom door and stepped inside, opening the medicine cabinet above the sink. Grabbing the acetaminophen bottle, she poured two pills out into her hand, popped them into her mouth, and swallowed them dry.

Replacing the bottle, she moved into the kitchen and drank a full glass of water to go with the medicine. Within the next thirty minutes, she would feel the aches beginning to leave and the headache disappear.

Up until that point, she had neglected to take any medicine because she was simply too lazy to grab it and too prideful to ask someone else to get it. Anna had shoved two ibuprofen tablets into Belle's hand when they'd originally brought her upstairs, but those had worn off ages ago. She chuckled to herself, thinking about how odd it was that she was willing to bend over backward to take care of the drive-in but not herself.

Also, something about a stabbing on your own business property put a fire under you.

She was determined to do her part.

Not only did she know the victim, but he also had always seemed like a kind person and a good businessman. She knew Dan was a great police officer and would do his best to investigate this crime to its fullest, but she wanted to also throw her hat in the ring.

Looking over her shoulder toward the apartment door that led down to the restaurant, she made sure no one was coming before she executed her next plan. Stepping to the side of the refrigerator, she cracked open the apartment's outside door which led to a metal fire escape. The set of stairs reached down to the ground floor.

Peeking out, she saw that the coast was clear. This side of the building was just outside the fence line that marked the parking area for movie showings. Also, the brick wall was backed up against the cypress trees of the bayou, giving her lots of coverage to come and go as she pleased without having to always trot through the bar and restaurant.

Dan and his fellow officer seemed to be out of sight and there was no sign of the police tape up near the screen that had been there the evening before. Dan had likely made quick work of the investigation, trudging through the evening into the early morning hours to make sure he felt satisfied in his search of the premises.

She wondered if they had, in fact, ever located the murder weapon. If the killer was smart, then he or she would have taken the weapon with them. She didn't expect to find anything herself, but she couldn't just sit around and wait.

Besides, getting outside and getting some fresh morning air would do her some good, she decided. Opening the door further, she stepped out onto the metal staircase.

"Going somewhere?" a male voice came from behind her.

"Yikes," she squeaked, turning and recognizing her friendly resident ghost peeking out through the brick wall of the building. "Why do you have to pop up like that?" she groaned.

"Sorry, it's not like I make much sound moving around."

He was right. He didn't have footsteps or the shuffle of clothing to accompany his movements, meaning he could just pop up anywhere. If he concentrated hard enough and exuded enough spiritual energy, he could move things in the physical world—but it took a lot out of him. He usually had to *recharge* as it were after any kind of activity like that.

It seemed even ghosts had physical limitations of some sort.

"What are you doing, anyway?" Belle shot out, pointing a finger at him.

"I could ask you the same thing," he huffed, coming out of the wall and floating on thin air beside the stairway.

Belle rolled her eyes. "None of your business."

"If you're looking for the murder weapon, don't bother," he said.

Belle rose both eyebrows and clasped her hands. "They found it?"

Harlem shook his head. "No."

Belle's expression dropped in confusion. "Huh?"

"No, they didn't find it," he paused, narrowing his gaze at her. His mouth twitched up into a mischievous smile. "I did."

CHAPTER FIVE

"It's just up the road," Harlem informed Belle as she followed him down into the front parking lot. The drive-in had two lots. The back one was surrounded by a high fence and was where people could pay to park and watch the nightly movies. The front lot was for restaurant guests who weren't planning on watching the movie on the big screen—although, Belle often showed old movies on a smaller projection screen inside as well.

Pausing, the ghost turned to face her. "You should probably take your car," he suggested.

"Why? Didn't you just say it was up the road?"

"Yes, but you've also been sick. I think it would be a safer bet if you took your car."

Belle rolled her eyes again. "You're starting to sound like Valerie, you know?"

"And your sister would kill me . . . again . . . if I didn't make sure you were safe," he said.

"Great. That's all I need is a ghostly escort," she joked, following his advice and walking over to her car. Getting in, they pulled out of the parking lot and up the road into the rural bayou area just beyond the drive-in.

"Here. Stop here," he instructed, pointing to an oddly shaped lump just off the side of the road.

Belle did as he said, squinting at the strangely shaped item. It looked like moss growing on a huge stone or something of the like. "What is that?"

"You'll see," he said.

Getting out of the car, Belle felt silently relieved that she'd taken the car as Harlem had suggested. While the pain meds were kicking in, she could feel just how worn out her body was from fighting the illness. Even just driving a little ways down the road had taken its toll.

Following the ghost toward the edge of the road,

she started to make sense of what she was seeing. The dead giveaway was the black side view mirror sticking out. "It's a car?" she exclaimed. By the looks of it, the vehicle was partially submerged in the swampy water, covering the wheels at the very least.

"That's right, but that isn't all," he said, motioning to the murky water.

Bending over, she saw the morning sunlight glint against something metal in the water. "A dagger," she practically shouted, her voice echoing off the trees. The water around it had a mild red tinge, indicating that there may have been blood on the blade at one point.

However, it didn't look like just any dagger. It had some strange lines carved into the blade, crisscrossing over one another and forming into the shape of a pentagram near the hilt. The handle seemed to be carved into the shape of black skulls stacked one atop the other. Even through the slight grime of the water, Belle could see that each of them had a pair of fangs—not unlike a vampire.

"A steel blade hewn with a technique where the smith folds the metal over itself again and again, creating a very thin, but very strong edge. The hilt is carved from black ivory."

Belle couldn't help lifting one eyebrow in a show of interest. "You sure seem to know a whole lot about this thing. Don't tell me you committed this murder," she joked.

Harlem chuckled. "Hardly. No, what I'm saying is that I'm familiar with this type of item."

Belle raised an eyebrow, not particularly liking the direction this train of thought was taking.

"This is a ritual dagger used in some voodoo, hoodoo, and folk magic practices. It's a very expensive piece."

"I bet."

"Not to mention, I think this one is fairly old."

Belle looked up at the black and white flickering face. "How can you tell that?"

"More of a gut feeling than anything else."

Shoving her hand into her pajama bottom pocket, she brought out her smartphone she'd brought along.

"Calling the police?" Harlem asked.

"Not until I get a few pictures," she admitted, opening her camera app. Narrowing the viewfinder on the blade, she snapped a few at different angles. Once she was satisfied with that, she looked at Harlem again, dreading to ask the question on her mind. "So, you said that this dagger is something used in rituals? Does that mean . . ." she let her voice trail off.

Harlem hesitated, but then eventually nodded. "That's right. I think we have some more black magic mixed in with this murder again."

"Where the heck have you been?" Anna demanded, seeing her sister walk in the front door of the restaurant. "And you were with her?" she continued, seeing Harlem float in behind Belle.

"Ugh, I already got scolded by Dan. I don't need it from you, too," she insisted, holding up a hand for Anna to be quiet.

"Dan? Why did you talk to Dan? Were you all the way down at the station?"

"No," she groaned. Pulling out her phone, Belle opened her photo gallery and set her phone on the counter as she went behind the bar. Grabbing a glass tumbler, she filled it with seltzer water and sipped it. "Have a look for yourself."

Using her finger to scroll through the images, Anna's eyes widened. "You found the murder weapon?"

"Correction. I found the murder weapon," Harlem chimed in.

"He's right, but I told Dan I found them since he doesn't know Harlem exists."

"I'm sure he would believe you if you told him," Harlem noted.

"No," the sisters said in unison.

"And what's this?" Anna asked, pointing at a mossy picture.

"A car. According to Dan, it belonged to Jason Dobbs." In a town as small as Sunken Grove, the police had little trouble identifying local cars or license plates from the small number of citizens.

"So, let me get this straight? The murderer drove the victim's car off the road, hid it under some moss and plants, and then dropped the murder weapon there?"

Belle shrugged. "Maybe?"

"There were tires marks on the pavement," Harlem chimed in. He'd had a much longer time to examine the scene up close.

Belle was sure that if she wasn't feeling so under the weather, that she too would have noticed. Anna, having as keen an eye for detail as anyone, would have as well.

"So, you think Jason crashed?" Anna asked.

"I think he may have been forced off the road somehow. Then, when he got out, the killer came after him with the knife. Jason ran into the bayou and ended up behind the movie screen before the killer finally caught up with him," Harlem deduced, a look of pride twinkling in his eye.

"That makes more sense, I suppose. But why leave the murder weapon there with the car where it would surely be found?" Belle pointed out.

Scrolling backward in the pictures, Anna looked at

the images of the knife again. She frowned as she examined it.

"Is something wrong?" Belle asked.

Anna didn't answer right away and instead took a moment to collect her thoughts before diving in with an answer. "I can't know for sure, but I think I've seen this knife somewhere before."

"You have?" Harlem and Belle responded together.

Anna nodded, setting the phone down. "I think it is from the little voodoo gift shop in town. The one owned by Payton Shaw."

CHAPTER SIX

While Belle, feeling completely wiped out from the morning's excitement, headed up to bed, Anna started making plans to visit Payton at his shop that day. Harlem, of course, insisted on tagging along. Anna was glad for the company. More so, she was glad to have his knowledge on board. Seeing as Harlem had owned a voodoo shop of his own in the French Quarter of New Orleans when he was alive, she figured he would know how to best read Payton and figure out more about this blade.

Where had it come from? Did it have some sort of significance? Was this crime related to some sort of dark folk magic, or was the weapon of choice purely random?

Somehow, Anna felt like the latter wasn't true.

With the history of strange murders and occurrences in town, she couldn't help but believe that this was another paranormal event in the mix.

On the way into town, Harlem explained his knowledge about the blade to Anna. "You don't think that Dan will be upset that you're going off and doing a little digging on your own?" he asked.

"Why would he be? I mean, I'm not tampering with evidence or obstructing any of his procedures, am I?" Anna said. She realized she was justifying her current actions, much in the way her own younger sister usually did.

In past murder cases, Anna had been the one to be hesitant to do any sort of digging. She often tried to talk her sister out of sticking her nose in where it didn't belong. However, over the months, Anna realized that she had just as much curiosity, if not more, than her sister.

The more important element here was the supernatural occurrences around these cases. While Dan and Valerie both practiced voodoo and folk magic as their religion of choice, proper police procedure simply didn't allow room for that kind of explanation in a report.

Therefore, Anna felt it was her place to do a little digging. "Dan doesn't have a ghost detective for a sidekick," she managed an answer.

"A ghost detective? Is that what I am now?"

Anna smirked. "Well, you kind of are."

"It does have a nice ring to it," he agreed.

Driving down Main Street, Anna pulled off to the side of the road and parked in front of Shaw's House of Voodoo which was located on the lower floor of a three-story building. The top floors were rooms for rent with a wrap around balcony looking out. The shop itself had a purposefully tattered look. The blood red painted walls and forest green shudders were peeling and cracked. Moss grew down from the awning and a circular neon sign hung out at an angle.

Getting out of the car, she walked in the open front door. The scent of musty air and aging wood immediately greeted her, accompanied by the thick stench of incense. The shop had shelf after shelf of trinkets, skulls, and jars along the wall. The ceiling as well was completely covered with products hanging from the rafters.

Accompanying the regularly creepy voodoo items were postcards, Louisiana branded souvenirs, and a whole section of t-shirts all stacked up one upon the other.

Harlem whistled. "Wow, and I thought my shop was cluttered."

"Welcome, welcome," Payton announced, stepping out of the back room wearing a long draping green shawl, a sparkly turban, and enough jewelry to sink a pirate ship. While he looked a little kooky on the outset, Anna knew he was just a sweet and gentle-hearted as they come.

Ever since her first few encounters with the supernatural, she had come into the shop looking for protective charms. She had, of course, not told a single soul that she had done so—or that she wore a protective pentagram necklace under her clothes. Not even Harlem knew.

"Ah, Anna. How lovely to see you, my darling."

"Hi, Payton. How is business?"

He flipped his hands up. "The same as ever. Can't complain." Waltzing over behind the jewelry counter he passed his hand over the glass case. "Looking for anything in particular? See anything you fancy?"

Harlem looked at her with a raised eyebrow. "He sure seems to know you. How many times have you been in here?"

Anna ignored him and smiled at the shop owner. "Actually, Payton, I'm not here to shop today."

"Oh, there is always time to shop," he said, always playing the salesman. "How about this black skull bead rosary? Beautiful craftsmanship along with the strength of a blessing upon it," he offered, showing a necklace that was made up completely of tiny hand-carved beads.

She had to admit, it was enticing. However, she put up her hands to ward off the sale. "No, no. I'm here for another reason." She took out her phone to which she'd transferred all of the pictures Belle had taken and showed an image of the dagger to him. "Do you have one of these in stock?" she asked, not wanting to tip him off to the fact that it was connected to a murder.

Payton, leaned in so close that Anna thought his nose would touch the screen. His eyebrows went up and he smiled. "A dagger, Anna? What in the world would you need that for?"

She rolled her eyes. "I don't, but do you have one?"

"I did have one that looked exactly like this, as a matter of fact."

"You did?" she pressed, eager to hear more.

"But I'm afraid I just sold it recently."

Anna's jaw dropped. "To whom?"

"Now, let me think," he said, humming quietly and tapping one gold ringed finger against his chin. "Ah, yes. I remember, now. It was to that trucker fellow. William Percy."

Anna scrunched up her eyebrows. She'd only met William Percy in passing. He had a hefty beer gut, a scraggly white beard, and tattoos all up and down his arms. He hardly seemed like someone who would want a ritual dagger. On the other hand, if he simply thought it looked cool, he might have picked it up.

The only other thing she knew about William was that he had an alcohol problem. Dan complained about having to pick him up on multiple occasions for disturbing the peace while intoxicated.

Certainly, he couldn't be the killer, could he? She supposed if he was driving drunk and accidentally forced Jason Dobbs off the road, maybe he wasn't thinking straight and went after the victim with the knife to keep him from reporting him to the police. After all, a DUI was no little thing. William could have his license taken away and incur other penalties as well depending on his history.

"William Percy bought it?" she asked for confirmation

"With cash," Payton added.

Anna thought for a second, gathering her thoughts. If he paid with cash, it meant there was no digital paper trail connecting a credit or debit card to the purchase. "Do you have a record of the sale?" she asked, wanting to be dead certain that William was the one who'd purchased the weapon.

"Does it look like I keep track of things like that?" Payton asked, motioning to the cluttered and dusty shop around them.

"You don't keep a ledger of your inventory and sales?" she pressed, thinking that it was a normal and responsible thing for a business owner to do. Even Belle, who hadn't always been the most organized in the past, kept detailed records of the drive-in's purchases and sales.

"Look, Anna, I've been running this business for fifteen years. I just buy up merchandise when I stumble across it—almost at random. I see something interesting or odd that will look good here in the shop, I buy it and then put it on the shelf with a marked-up price. I never write any of it down and I don't keep track of who buys it."

"You don't even have a receipt or something?"

"All sales are final." He indicated the worn sign behind the counter. He raised an eyebrow. "Why is it so important anyway?"

"No reason," she spat out quickly. "Well, good luck with everything." She figured she wasn't going to get any more helpful information from him and it was time to leave. She had the buyer's name and that would have to do for now.

Turning around to leave, she noticed that Harlem was nowhere in sight like he'd wandered off during the conversation. Where could he have gone?

CHAPTER SEVEN

Harlem had grown disinterested in the conversation between Anna and the shopkeeper. Tracking down the purchaser of a knife didn't seem to prove anything. While it did narrow down some of the possibilities in this situation, it seemed to him that the sale of the weapon in question didn't prove anything one way or another—especially if the shopkeeper couldn't provide evidence or proof that anyone had purchased it.

Perhaps Payton was telling the truth, and this trucker, William Percy, had purchased the item. Maybe, even, William was the killer.

But what was the motive or reasoning for the killing? Without some more solid evidence, it was an empty theory at best.

However, what if William had lost the knife or it had gotten stolen? What if it had been stolen from the shop proper and Payton didn't want to admit that he was a victim of theft out of some weird sense of pride? Harlem, having been a member of the voodoo goods business in his life, had met weirder shop owners than that.

The last and final thought that Harlem had was maybe the knife had never been sold at all and Payton was lying about it.

If there was one thing Harlem had learned in the time since his death, investigating his own murder as well as others, was that you considered *all* the options before formulating a hypothesis.

Since this particular murder seemed to be so open-ended, with no true and hardened suspects yet, he decided he needed to do a little more digging—digging that only he as a ghost could do.

These were all the thoughts running through Harlem's head as he floated out of the main room of the shop and into the storage area in the back.

Moving into the room, he couldn't help but stop

dead cold with his eyes wide. If the shop itself looked cluttered, the storage space was like a disaster zone. Boxes upon boxes sat on atop the other in haphazard towers that threatened to collapse at any moment. Many of them looked squished or even soggy in spots, a couple bits of mold showing through. It was proof that this place never got cleaned. Added on top and in between all the boxes were random pieces of merchandise including candles, crystals, poppet dolls, and more. Layering over all of it was a thick layer of cobwebs.

Just by looking at it, you'd assume that no one had been back here in the past thirty years. Payton wasn't kidding when he'd indicated he wasn't one for organization. It was little surprise he didn't keep a record of inventory or sales.

How the man managed his taxes at the end of each year, Harlem had no idea.

Running a small shop like this was no easy task and required dedication and organization. Had Payton opened this business in the French Quarter, he would have gone under within a year, most likely.

Shaking his head in disbelief, Harlem squeezed

through the area and toward the wooden door marked "office" at the back of the room. He knew he didn't need to squeeze or dodge away from the hanging cobwebs, seeing as he'd just float through them, but it was a basic reflex left over from when he was alive.

Passing through the doorway, he entered the office space. This time, upon seeing the stacks of papers, overfilled filing cabinets, long spent wax candles, and cobwebs, he was far less surprised. This Payton Shaw character was an interesting fellow. In Harlem's experience, people with cluttered living and work spaces like this had cluttered lives.

They were often the kind to harbor deep secrets. Sometimes those secrets were little more than low self-esteem or familial issues. On the other hand, the clutter and cobwebs could be a cover-up for something more sinister.

He'd seen it among his own community of shopkeepers in New Orleans. He was sure small-town Louisiana was no different in that regard.

Floating around the desk, he noticed a half-eaten beignet sitting on a wrinkled napkin and a sludgy cold residue inside a skull shaped mug that had once been coffee, no doubt. Harlem hoped that those were from that morning, but somehow, he doubted it.

The next thing that caught his eye was the stack of mail, unopened bills and such, piled on one side. He wondered if it would be worth the spiritual energy to move the items and got through it all. However, reading the top envelope, he realized he wouldn't have to.

The envelope was stamped in big red letters. *Eviction Notice.*

The kicker was the return address. It named the office of Jason Dobbs as the sender.

"He lied about sales being good," Harlem said, materializing in the driver seat of the car.

"Ack! Why do you do that?" Anna complained, putting a hand on her chest to slow the beating of her heart. "Stop popping up like that all the time."

"Sorry about that. I just got excited is all," he admitted.

Anna shook her head, sliding her key into the ignition. "Where the heck did you disappear to? What good are you if you're not eavesdropping on the conversation?"

"I heard most of it but got bored."

She raised an eyebrow. "So, you just wandered off?"

"Not exactly. I did a little more digging that only a *ghost* could do while you finished up with Payton."

"Oh?" Putting the car in reverse, she backed out onto the street.

"I went back into the guy's office. I can tell you one thing, that place is a horrific mess."

"Is that all you learned?" she said, continuing down the road toward her apartment above an empty shop space. Tourists were already out and walking around, looking in store windows and grabbing a bite to eat at the little cafes.

"No, that isn't all I learned."

"So?"

"On his desk, there was a letter of eviction."

"What?" she blurted out. "You mean an eviction notice?"

"That's right. It seems that he won't be holding onto that shop space for much longer, and I don't envy whoever has to clean it all out if he decides to just leave it as is. Some people do that, you know?"

"So, he is just putting on a show? Ignoring it?"

"That's my guess. Otherwise, he just never looks at his mail and therefore missed it."

"Okay, so what does all of this have to do with the murder."

To this question, Harlem smirked proudly. "The letter was sent from the office of Jason Dobbs."

Anna's jaw dropped. "You're kidding me."

"Nope. It seems Jason owns the property and Payton was likely behind on his rent."

"Sheesh, I knew Jason Dobbs owned some of the property around town. Belle told me that. I guess evicting people who don't pay is just part of the job."

"That's right, but what if someone was in a desperate

situation and blamed Jason for being evicted. Why they might even take a dagger from their own shop and kill the guy."

Anna slowed the car and pulled over the side of the road, so she could look Harlem in the eye. "Wait a minute. You think that he lied about selling the dagger?"

"He doesn't have any sort of record or proof that he sold it, does he?"

"I suppose not, but murder?"

"Look, I know the thought crossed your mind," Harlem pointed out.

Anna turned one corner of her mouth down and squinted at him, mostly upset that he was right. "Okay, okay. That is one potential theory."

"It's the best one we have so far. He had possession of the dagger at one time and has a potential motive for the killing."

Taking her foot off the brake, she pulled back out into the street to continue her drive. "Okay, we'll keep that theory in mind. In the meantime," she thought out loud, her voice trailing off.

"What?"

"The only way to know for sure if he had the dagger and didn't sell it is to track down William Percy."

CHAPTER EIGHT

After retreating to her apartment for a while and hopping online, Anna was able to track down an address for William Percy. While he was a man in his late forties, he was pretty active on social media as well, mostly updating followers about where he was going to be that week. Being a trucker, he was often not in town. He spent weeks at a time on the road, hauling merchandise across the country to various states.

It became apparent that he was a private trucker. He took commissions and jobs from various contract employers instead of working for one specific trucking company. He could be traveling anywhere at any time—always on a different route.

This kind of job also meant he owned his own truck

to haul the various loads. Anna had to silently admire the type of work ethic, time, and dedication such a difficult job might present. It was much harder than her own job helping to manage that drive-in theater with her sister and Valerie.

Speaking of which, she realized that she would probably be in for a scolding later that day from Valerie for not being there all morning to help with the set up of that night's vampire flick—*Dance of the Vampire Brides.*

While she still wasn't overly excited to see this next movie, she did like the idea of the vampires being women in this one instead of a man. However, she wasn't holding her breath. She was sure it would be just a cheesy and over the top as the last ones.

"You've got the address. Are we ready to go?" Harlem asked, floating back and forth in the tiny apartment with impatience.

Anna had seen tigers pacing back and forth, but this was something new. She couldn't help but chuckle at him.

"What is so funny?"

"You. You're just raring to go."

"Yes, I'm getting anxious to figure this out."

Anna scrunched her eyebrows together. "Oh? Why is that? This isn't any different than some of the other murder cases we've faced."

"That's just it. The other cases we've helped solve always have something paranormal involved."

"Well, yeah. If you're helping to do some snooping, of course, there is," she joked.

He stopped his pacing and looked down at her unamused. "You know what I mean."

"Yeah, yeah. I'm just trying to keep things lighthearted, you know?"

"What about you? Why are you so laid back about this case? You're usually chomping at the bit, either to get the case solved or to get your sister uninvolved."

Anna sighed. It was true. Seeing Belle get all mixed up in dangerous and supernatural events around Sunken Grove bothered her. She'd spent part of Belle's teenage years caring for her sister after their parents died. She was overprotective in some ways. Wanting to stop her from getting mixed up in murder . . . and potentially worse situations . . . was almost a knee-jerk response.

However, this time around Belle was laid up sick in bed. Despite having gone out that morning to do some investigating, she just didn't have the energy to keep going.

It made Anna more invested in the case. She realized her own level of curiosity wasn't so different from her sister's, especially when her sister wasn't as involved. Finally looking up at Harlem again, she shrugged one shoulder. "This case may not have a paranormal element at all, you know?"

"But it was a voodoo ritual dagger used to kill him," Harlem reminded her.

"Yeah, but our two suspects might not have used any voodoo or folk magic in the killing. It may have just been a matter of ease using the knife."

Harlem sighed. "Okay, okay, but I don't want to rule it out just yet."

"Don't worry. We won't," she replied, looking back to the computer screen. "I just need to find out if William Percy is in town or on the road, but it looks like he hasn't posted in the last two weeks or so."

"So, maybe he's on the road, then."

"No. It seems like he posts more when he is on the road. Taking pictures of places he has been. The weird thing is, hardly any of these have any likes or comments on them. It's like he was posting all of this for his own benefit."

"Or he was hoping for a little attention."

"He could be lonely. As far as I can tell he doesn't have any family to speak of. Also, trucking is a pretty lonely job. Not to mention, he isn't part of a company, so it isn't like he'd even have fellow employees or drivers to be buddies with."

Harlem folded his arms. "So sad."

"Anyway, I say we go down to this address he has listed and see if he's at home. At the very least he can help us clear up the little matter of who had the dagger."

"Where is this place?" Harlem asked, leaning down to have a look at the computer screen.

Anna clicked over to a new tab and entered the address, pulling up a digital map. "Looks like he's about ten minutes outside of town on a bayou road.

Could be an old farmhouse or plantation. That's generally what's around, you know?"

Harlem hesitated, his initial eagerness to get out the door fading. "I'm well aware."

"What's wrong?" she insisted to know.

"Think of this. What if he *is* the killer? Are we going out to a secluded spot to ask him about the murder weapon? Come on, that can't be very smart. If Belle was doing this, you'd insist on either going along or calling the cops."

Anna shook her head. "Stop worrying. It's not like I'm going in there and asking if he murdered anyone. I could just say I had hoped to buy the dagger from the shop and heard he'd purchased before I got to it. I'll ask if I can buy it from him."

Harlem looked at her with a skeptical frown.

"I'm taking you along, aren't I?" she defended herself, feeling more and more like her sister.

He held out his hands in protest. "What am I going to do?"

"You're a ghost. Scare him off if he tries anything."

Pursing his lips, Harlem floated toward the door. "I hope this works out the way you planned. The last thing we need is another body."

"Or another ghost haunting the drive-in with you," she joked.

Harlem was not amused.

CHAPTER NINE

The sky had turned gray as morning shifted into the afternoon. Driving out of town, tiny droplets of rain dotted along the windshield of Anna's car. Above the cypress trees, the gray clouds rolled in looking like menacing towers filled with water.

"Looks like we've got a storm coming," Harlem noted, leaning forward in his seat to look out at the darkening sky.

"It would seem so."

"Perfect weather for a murder," he said.

Anna rolled her eyes. "No one is getting murdered. Honestly, he may not even be at home. Then, you won't have to worry anymore about it."

"We can only hope," he agreed.

The real worry would be if William bought the dagger. If so, did he have a motive to use it against Jason Dobbs?

"Also, I sent a text to Valerie saying I was heading out this direction. If I randomly go missing, everyone will know something is up. Also, you can always tell my sister what happened to me if anything does."

"Nothing is *going* to happen to you," he argued, not liking the way she was talking. He knew she was just pushing his buttons. Anna had originally been pretty standoffish to him, seeing as he was a ghost and all. However, as she'd grown more comfortable and they'd become friends, she'd also become more playful. She sure knew how to rub him the wrong way if she wanted to, though.

He was only now realizing that he felt protective of the drive-in sisters, especially Anna. They got mixed up with so many creepy happenings, he just hoped that his knowledge of the occult could help them out.

He never wanted to see either of them hurt, or

worse, on account of one of these strange occurrences.

It didn't help that Sunken Grove seemed like a breeding ground for paranormal activity. In his life's studies, he became aware of the fact that certain areas and locations throughout the world had a thinner veil between the living and the dead. Sunken Grove seemed to be one such place, which is why it drew in some of the more daring tourists looking to do a little ghost hunting.

Harlem couldn't help chuckle at the thought. What if those ghost hunters knew that he, a real ghost, was just oh so close to them?

"What's funny?" Anna asked, having heard him laugh quietly to himself.

"Oh, nothing. Just thinking what would happen if a crew of ghost hunters ever came to the drive-in."

Anna smiled at this thought. "We'd have to put on a show for them. We are in the business of entertaining, after all."

This time, Harlem laughed out loud. "So true." He was honestly glad for the turn in mood. He was already beginning to feel more secure about this little trip. Somehow, it seemed like things would work out okay.

"I think this is the turn off right here," Anna noted, gripping the wheel and navigating the car onto the dirt backroad. If the rain really started to come down, that road would turn into mud. It would be harder to get back out.

She tried not to think along those lines.

In a matter of minutes, a two-story farmhouse came into view. The white paint was peeling and yellowed in spots and shingles were missing from the roof. It looked like something out of one of Belle's movies. A shiver danced up Anna's spine as she parked out front.

Parked in the trees just off to the side was a mini-van. Clearly, someone was home.

"A mini-van? Doesn't seem much like a trucker's choice of vehicle," Harlem commented.

"Maybe he has family visiting?"

"I thought you said it didn't seem like he had any family?"

"Maybe I was wrong. People don't put *everything* on social media." Opening her door, she climbed out, quickly followed by Harlem.

Just as she had suspected, the rain had begun coming down harder. Large fat droplets plunked around them, riding along the top of the dirt yard for a few seconds before settling into the soil. The house had an enclosed wrap around porch, which made Anna feel a little more comfortable since it meant she wouldn't have to stand out in the rain while knocking on a stranger's door.

She'd seen William in passing and knew who he was, but she'd never once spoken a word to him.

"Now remember. Be careful," Harlem told her in a hushed tone, even though no one would be able to hear him. "At the first sign of trouble, make a run for it."

Anna shook her head. "I'm sure nothing bad is going to happen. We'll just ask our questions and then get out of here."

A rumble of thunder overhead ushered in a massive downpour, coating the entire yard and surrounding bayou area in a curtain of water. A second later, the echo of a familiar sound came from somewhere within the building, barely audible above the sound of the rain.

If she wasn't mistaken, Anna could swear it was a baby crying. That couldn't be right, could it?

No turning back now. Taking a deep breath, Anna balled her hand into a fist and knocked on the door. She stood there quietly for a moment, her heart beating against her rib cage, as she attempted to listen to what was happening inside.

She could make out the muted words, *who could* and *take care of,* drowned out by the rain.

A second later, the door opened. Much to Anna's surprise, she was faced with a woman of about twenty-nine or thirty staring back at her through the wire screen door with a baby in her arms. "Hello? Can I help you?" she asked, shifting the crying baby to her other hip.

Anna hesitated, not sure what to say. "I'm sorry. I think I have the wrong address. I was looking for William Percy?"

"Sorry, he don't live here no more. It's just me, my

kids, and the husband when he ain't working on people's septic tanks round here."

Anna couldn't help cringing at the job.

"Trust me, doll. It ain't a pretty job. He comes home stinkin' worse than the cat box most nights, but it pays well, and he enjoys it for what it is." She shifted the baby's weight again, trying to get a better hold of the red-faced child. Thankfully, he was quieting down as the mother rocked him lovingly.

Anna felt a little sad for the woman. She had a sweet face with rosy red round cheeks and even a slight hint of a smile, despite how exhausted she looked. Besides the child in her arms, a toddler appeared to be playing with a tower of blocks in the living room beyond.

"That blasted thunder woke him up from his nap. Right when I was about to start unpackin' the kitchen boxes, too. I can never get much done around here before hubby gets home. Thankfully, he takes the kids off my hands for a few hours, so I can get more done like unpackin' and cleanin'. But sometimes I'm even too tired for all that and end up soakin' in the tub and readin' a book, you know?"

Anna gave a sympathetic smile, happy to know the woman had an attentive husband. "That's nice of him."

"We've been slow goin' of it, getting all moved in and such. We were just thrilled to finally get a place to stay that wasn't a dirty motel. Hubby's been workin' for over three weeks now at this new job, so we just moved in 'bout a week ago after that last guy got kicked out. I'd say I was sorry for him, but I'd be lying. I'm all too happy to finally have a place for my kids."

Anna blinked a few times, thinking things through. "Oh? So, the last tenant got kicked out?"

"That's right. His name was Bill or Will or something. He wasn't too happy to be leaving and made our move-in day pretty difficult. Cursin' and kickin' about in front of my kids. It's a bad example, ya know?"

"I don't doubt it. He was really that much trouble?"

"You better believe it, hon'. The police had to come and escort him off the land. 'course, he'd already had his things packed up and out before then, but thought he'd put up one final stink before kickin' off.

I haven't the faintest idea what happened to him after that."

"Wow, that sounds hard."

"Yeah, last night I got worried, too. I thought he'd come back. I swear I saw someone movin' about outside, stalkin' among the trees. I was about to call that chief again when my hubby said not to. He's got a shotgun and said he'd scare anyone who came callin' off. Luckily, whoever it was ended up leavin', but I swear it was that fella'."

"This was William Percy?" Anna pressed.

"Yeah, that's his name. He was the previous tenant. According to our landlord, he got evicted two weeks ago. They took a week to clean the place up, and then that's when we moved in."

Anna hummed quietly, thinking this all seemed like quite the coincidence. She had a good bet on who the landlord was. "And who is renting the place to you?" she asked.

"Oh, a real nice fella' named Jason Dobbs. He's a real sweetheart."

Anna smiled, eyeballing her invisible partner with a knowing eye. "Well, thanks for your time, anyway."

"Are you a resident here?" the woman asked before Anna could leave. "We don't know a whole lot a' folks here yet."

"Yes, I am. My name is Anna-Lee Francis."

The woman's eyes went wide, and her face erupted into a smile. "Oh, my goodness. Are you one of those sisters who owns that drive-in?"

Anna was surprised that the woman knew about her and the drive-in. Tilting her head, she smiled. "That's right. My sister owns it and I help run it."

"Oh, that's just amazin'. I'd heard about it from the guy who runs the motel. Hubby and I have been talkin' about going out to that place for a date night once we get settled. We just love old movies. I mean, if it don't cost too much or nothin'. Not to mention finding a babysitter."

"Well, maybe I could babysit for you," Anna offered before she knew what she was doing. "And I'm sure Belle would be more than willing to give you guys two complimentary tickets for your first time."

"Oh, you're a sweetheart. Really?"

Anna nodded, knowing she couldn't back out of it now. "Once you guys get settled, just give me a call over at the drive-in during business hours and we can work something out."

"Why, that sounds lovely, hon'. That sounds just lovely."

CHAPTER TEN

"You? Babysitting?" Belle asked with her mouth wide open.

Anna sat on the arm of the couch in her sister's upstairs apartment above the restaurant. Belle was all wrapped up in multiple layers of blankets, a cup of lemon honey tea clasped in her hands to help keep her warm. The rainstorm had brought an uncomfortable chill into the room. Meanwhile, Harlem stood off to the side with his arms folded, listening to the two girls talk.

"I know, I know. It sort of just slipped out, and she seemed like such a sweet woman."

"I think you're just a sucker," Belle teased.

"Now, that's rude," Anna retorted.

"Not to mention, you offered free tickets without my approval first," she declared, turning her head up, closing her eyes, and sticking her lips out in an exaggerated pouty face.

"Hey, am I a manager here or not?" the older sister defended herself, taking her sister's joke a little too personally.

"Hey, hey, hey, can we talk about the matter at hand?" Harlem asked, diverting the sisters' attention away from the antics of babysitting and business management. While he usually didn't mind the sisterly squabbles and playful bickering, he was growing more concerned about this case the deeper they got into it.

"He's right. We now have two suspects with the same motive," Anna mentioned.

"One who has already been evicted and another who is going to be soon?" Belle asked for clarification, going over the facts her sister had already shared with her earlier.

"That's right," Anna replied. "While Jason Dobbs

was apparently just doing his job as a property owner and real estate agent, some of his tenants might not feel the same. To them, they're either having their home or their livelihood taken out from under them."

As Anna laid out the facts, Harlem started his pacing again.

"But was he just doing his job?" Belle asked, grabbing a tissue from the nearby box and blowing her nose.

"What do you mean?" Anna pressed.

"I mean, are we sure Jason wasn't using any kind of dishonest business tactics?" She tossed the tissue across the room, landing it in the wastebasket near the window.

"I thought Jason was a friend of yours," the older sister asked with one upturned eyebrow.

"I wouldn't call him a friend, necessarily. I only interacted with him while I was in the midst of buying this property. He seemed like a nice guy. Sort of quiet, but professional."

"So, what makes you suspect that he was being dishonest?"

She shrugged. "I don't, necessarily. I just wondered if there was more to this whole thing than we thought. I think killing your landlord for evicting you is a pretty extreme measure. Like you said, Jason was just doing his job."

Harlem's stopped his pacing and looked at the sisters. "It may seem extreme, but if you're in a desperate enough situation, people are willing to do most anything."

"I guess," Belle said skeptically.

"By the sound of it, William Percy did not take well to the eviction. He had to be removed from the property, according to the new owners."

"That's right. It sounded like Dan handled the situation himself," Anna added.

"Well, maybe we should call and ask him about it," Belle offered.

"Ask me about what?" came a familiar gruff, yet comforting voice from the apartment's doorway.

"Sorry, I didn't knock. I heard you girls talking and thought you wouldn't mind me popping in," Dan said, walking over to the couch.

His dark bald head shimmered with water droplets, revealing that he'd just come in from the rain. Pulling a handkerchief from his breast pocket, he wiped them away.

"That's okay, Dan. It saves us from calling you," Belle beamed.

"Are we sure we want to tell him that you've been snooping, Anna?" Harlem asked, knowing that the police chief wouldn't be able to hear him.

Anna ignored this comment, knowing that discussing their findings with Dan was the right choice. Not only was he the chief of police in Sunken Grove, but he was also like family.

"What was it you girls were going to ask me?"

"About the woman living in William Percy's old place," Anna said, realizing she'd never even gotten the woman's name while she was there. How could she have been so foolish?

"You mean Diane Keen?" Dan asked.

Anna hesitated. "Honestly, I don't know her name."

Dan put his meaty fists on his hips. "Were you out there today?"

"Yes, I was. I was looking for William Percy," she admitted.

"Well, don't," he ordered, waving a finger at her.

Belle and Anna looked at one another with quizzical glances before turning their attention back to Dan. "Why not?" Anna asked.

"William has been emotionally unstable these past few weeks. He might be dangerous. I don't want you girls going anywhere near him. It's been hard enough to make sure Diane and her family are safe in that house."

"Is that because he's dangerous enough to hurt someone . . . maybe even commit murder?" Anna pressed, all too interested in this new snippet of information. If Dan suspected William, that was a big deal.

Dan frowned, his bushy eyebrows pushing together.

"Anna, have you been digging around where you shouldn't be?"

She put up her hands. "I'm sorry. I just recognized the dagger from Payton's shop, so I thought it wouldn't hurt for me to ask him about it."

Dan set his jaw. "You shouldn't have done that."

"Why? Because he's a suspect?" she asked forthwith—maybe not the best choice.

A low grunt of displeasure escaped his throat. Anna hadn't seen Dan get irritated with them like this before.

"I figured that out when I realized he was being evicted from his shop soon," Anna admitted.

"How did you learn that?" Dan exclaimed, shocked.

"I just did," she said, unwilling to reveal the truth.

Harlem rolled his eyes in the background.

"And I suppose he told you he sold that dagger to William Percy, huh?"

Anna hesitated. "Yes, sir."

"And then you went out to William's address only to find another family living there." Dan pinched the bridge of his nose for a second before continuing. "I'd expect something like that from Belle, but you, Anna?"

"Hey," Belle protested.

"I'm not trying to hurt your feelings or make you feel bad, but these people might be dangerous, okay?"

"I found the car and the dagger, didn't I?" Belle protested, knowing that no one here would have been able to find out as much as they had if Harlem hadn't shown her the dagger. Belle was the one who'd called it in.

"Yes, and I appreciated that. You did a very good job at calling me directly as soon as you'd found them." He turned his gaze back to Anna. "But going after a potentially dangerous person without even notifying me about the things you had learned wasn't smart," he scolded her.

"I told you so," Harlem added.

Anna, not appreciating being called out after she'd done so much work, folded her arms in a show of protest. She wasn't usually the type to go against rules or regulations, but this time she couldn't help feeling a little defensive. However, her conservative nature kept her from talking back unnecessarily. A part of her knew Dan was right.

It had been risky. Belle was usually the one to take on those situations.

"I know you girls have been a help in the past during other cases—especially seeing as there were some . . . elements . . . that I, as an officer, couldn't logically take head-on or add in my reports. Heaven knows my only other officer couldn't even fathom the idea of it." The girls knew he was referring to the potentially paranormal elements involved in almost every murder case that had come their way. "While part of me appreciates you girls and the help you've provided, I realize now I should have been firmer with you two. In this instance, there is no sign of anything strange involved with the murder. It's just that, a murder, and those can be more dangerous in many ways. Do you understand?"

The girls both nodded, not wanting to cause more of a conflict than there already was.

"Someone like William Percy is a loose cannon. He hasn't had a proper job in months. He fell behind on the payments of his semi-truck and it was repossessed."

Belle and Anna's jaws dropped. "You mean he lost his entire livelihood?" Belle asked.

"That's right. As a result, he also lost his home. He is a desperate man, and desperate men do wild and foolish things sometimes."

The sisters were quickly realizing that the clues were pointing to William. However, for Anna, she didn't want to count Payton out just yet. In her estimation, it was just as easy for the shopkeeper to use the unstable and down on his luck man as a scapegoat by claiming William had bought the knife—despite not having proof of the sale.

"The point is, we're on the lookout for William now. He hasn't appeared to be anywhere in town, as far as we can tell, so I've put an APB for the surrounding areas." He pointed at them again. "However, I don't want you girls going around looking for him or doing any other kind of investigating. Got it?"

"Got it," they said in subdued unison.

"If you see any sign of him near here, you call me first thing and steer clear of him."

They agreed, not wanting to worry the officer further.

"Okay, good. I've got to get out there and back to the search. I just wanted to check in on you girls." With a little wave and the return of his usual cheery smile, he disappeared out the door and down the stairs to the restaurant.

CHAPTER ELEVEN

After Dan left, there was a moment of awkward silence among the trio still in the apartment. Letting out a huff and setting down her nearly empty mug of tea on the coffee table, Belle threw the blankets over the back of the couch and used both hands to push herself up to a standing position.

"Hey, what do you think you're doing?" Anna argued, standing up herself to try and force her sister back down to rest.

"Well, I can't just sit here anymore. I've gotta do something," Belle insisted. The medicine had fully kicked in from earlier in the day and didn't seem to be wearing off. While she still felt a touch stuffy and feverish, she was feeling well enough to at least be up and around.

"Did you not hear what Dan just said? He doesn't want us involved anymore in this case."

"Hey, don't start scolding me. You were the one poking your nose into things this time," she reminded her older sister.

Anna's lips scrunched together tightly, turning white. Belle could tell her sister knew she was right. "Still, that doesn't give you the freedom to go out and start investigating now."

"She's right, Belle. You really shouldn't get involved in this case," Harlem added his two cents worth.

Belle looked around her sister at the ghost. "And why are you so concerned about this particular murder? I've never seen you get so worried before," she informed him.

"Look. It's just a gut feeling. I know that Dan thinks this whole thing is a cut and dry murder. He's worried about someone who was just in a place of desperation." He paused.

"But?" Belle pressed.

"But, I can't help but feel like there is something more

to this case. That is a ritual dagger and an old one at that. I don't know the weapon's history or potential supernatural power." He shook his head and placed his hands on his hips, looking down at his feet with a sigh. "All I know is what I feel. Call it a spirit's intuition if you will, but I can't help but feel there is some dark folk magic involved here somehow."

"Like what? I doubt William Percy has much experience in voodoo," Belle noted.

"Unless you're thinking it was Payton. He sells magic items, but does he know how to use them?" Anna added.

Harlem put up his hands. "I don't know, okay? I don't know for sure, but it is a feeling I have. I think all of us, including Dan, need to tread more carefully. We've approached every other case we've come across from the standpoint that there was something darker and unknown involved. We need to act the same here."

"So, are you saying we should continue investigating?" Anna inquired, raising an eyebrow.

"We don't have to go against anything Dan has

requested. We don't have to talk to Payton again or go looking for William."

"Then what?" Belle insisted.

Making sure he had their whole and undivided attention, he answered. "I think we need to visit an old friend of mine in New Orleans. She'll know something more about this dagger than I do."

"And what are you hoping she'll tell us?"

He hesitated, licking his lips. "Hopefully, nothing too horrible."

Somehow, Anna didn't like that answer. "So, basically, by just making a trip to learn more about the dagger, we aren't meddling in the investigation like Dan asked."

"That's right," he agreed. His gaze fell on Belle. "However, I don't think you should come, seeing as you've been sick."

"Well, that's good then, because I wasn't planning on going out and doing any investigating," she declared proudly, stepping into her flip-flops she'd had on the hardwood floor.

"You weren't?" Anna asked with a hint of surprise in her eyes.

"No, I had no intentions of doing that. I was only planning on going downstairs and helping Valerie and the waiters and waitresses get ready for this evening's guests." With that, she walked past them and down to the restaurant.

Belle didn't wait around to say goodbye to her sister and Harlem. She was getting tired of being treated like glass. She had a cold, so what? That didn't make her a frail waif.

She was aware that Valerie would argue with her as well, but she wasn't going to let it stop her. She knew her own limits and would head back to bed if she started feeling woozy again.

"What are you doing down here? Get back to bed," Valerie ordered, seeing Belle walk into the kitchen.

"Enough, Val. Just let me help down here. It's my business after all."

"You're sick, young lady."

"I feel fine," she insisted, going over to the sink and pumping foaming soap into her hands. With a vigor, she washed her hands to get rid of any of the germs. She'd been washing her hands nonstop that day whenever she got a chance. "I'm not going to do anything too strenuous, I promise."

Valerie pursed her lips, clearly unsure if this was a good idea. After a moment, she relented. "Alright, then, but the instant you start to feel ill, you're back up those stairs."

"I can handle myself," she promised, using a clean paper towel to dry her hands.

"Where is your sister? She'd been gone all day long and I've been here taking care of tonight's food prep alone."

Belle sighed. "She's had something come up. I should have told you," she said, covering for her sister.

Val put on a smile. "You've been sick, so I understand not wanting to run down here just for that. Anyway, it's fine. One of the waitresses can help me when they get in."

Belle glanced at the clock. It was about three. The

waitresses and waiters on shift for the evening would get there within the next half hour to start setting up the dining room. Many of them had been taught some of the cooking skills and recipes just for this type of occasion.

"Oh, by the way, we're running low on those blood patterned tablecloths we've been using. At least three got stained last night and I haven't been able to get around to washing them," Valerie informed the drive-in owner.

"Got it. Don't worry about it tonight. I've got a whole extra carton of them in the storage room," she informed her. "In fact, I'll go get them now."

"Just be careful going down there," Val said.

Belle tried not to roll her eyes. She'd been down in the basement storage area time and time again. While they kept their entire stock of food supply in the fridge, freezer, and walk-in pantry, all the props and decorations for the various events they hosted were in the basement.

Walking into the pantry, she knelt to grab the ring attached to the trap door to the basement and lifted it up. The open door revealed a set of concrete steps going down into the darkness below.

Belle worked hard to keep her business premises clean, even the basement which had a habit of accumulating dust. She tried to get down there at least once a week with the vacuum to suck up any dusty residue. Still, even with her efforts, the stairs managed to have a thin layer along the top by virtue of the room being underground and old.

Walking down the top few steps, she hit a switch on the wall that illuminated the stairway as well as the rest of the basement. Descending down, she was greeted by the familiar sight of shelves and storage drawers all labeled and organized perfectly. While a lot of the items were just silly Halloween decorations she'd collected through the years, others were collectibles or antiques. She had to make sure the items were well taken care of.

Coming the rest of the way down the steps, she walked across the room toward the drawers where she kept tablecloths. She had various colors and patterns for different occasions and party themes but was looking for the ones that were white with blood spatters for the vampire marathon.

It was as she was walking, passing the wall of large items such as full-size statues and fake coffins, that something out of the corner of her eye caught her attention. Turning to look, she noticed that one of the black coffins was on its back instead of standing up in its slot against the wall.

She knew she'd gotten out a few coffins to decorate for the week, but she didn't remember leaving one out. "How'd you get there?" she wondered out loud, walking over to it.

Could Anna or Valerie have pulled it down for some reason? No, that didn't make sense. Belle was generally the only person who came down here on her own. Anna only came down when Belle needed help bringing something up.

Shrugging, she decided not to let it bother her and just put it back upright. Grabbing the sides of the coffin, she groaned as she realized the coffin was much heavier than usual—as if something had been stored inside.

Letting it back down on the floor, she took a deep breath. Feeling her hands grow instantly ice cold, she hesitated with her hands hovering over the lid.

Did she dare open it? What could possibly be inside?

Knowing she didn't have much of a choice, she slowly and reluctantly grabbed the lid on either side and lifted it. As soon as she got it free, she felt her heart drop into her stomach.

A pale face with eyes wide in the stare of death looked up at her. Its hands were at its sides, but the fingers were clutching in claw-like shapes. A sense of unearthly horror and terror resided behind the face's expression.

She turned away, blinking a few times to clear her vision, just to make sure it was real. It took her a second to catch her breath, but then she looked back at it.

This time, she recognized the dead man.

It was the body of William Percy.

CHAPTER TWELVE

"What am I supposed to say to this lady? *Hi, I know your dead friend, Harlem. Hey, can you tell me about this knife?*" Anna complained, standing on a back street in the French Quarter of New Orleans. The rain had stopped before they arrived, leaving a cool and welcoming evening temperature in the air. As the sun set across the horizon of buildings, the active lights of the lively city came up to a fervent glow.

"No, not necessarily," Harlem answered, taking in the old sites. He hadn't been to *Marilla's Shop of Voodoo Wares* since he was alive. The circular red and black sign that hung on the door was a warm sight to see, but also a little sad—a reminder of something that once was and would never be again.

He had not bothered informing Anna that Marilla

and he had once been lovers and that he still sometimes pined after her even in death.

It was an unnecessary detail that would only complicate things.

If he hadn't felt learning about the dagger was absolutely key, he probably wouldn't have even suggested coming down here to see her.

"Oh, well. Let's get this over with," Anna sighed, pushing through the front door and hearing the bell chime above her head.

Harlem floated in behind her, staying close and keeping his eyes peeled. For all he knew, Marilla wasn't even here at the moment and one of her many temporary shop assistants could be manning the counter. Part of him hoped for the latter.

He didn't get his wish.

"Good evening, my dear," an elegant woman greeted Anna, sweeping out from behind a curtain of beads dressed in a long flowing red and black gown. Sequins sparkled in the pattern of swirls and skulls along the thin fabric that hugged her curves suggestively. Her midnight black hair draped over her shoulders, a glint of silver ribbons tied in the strands.

Harlem, if he had a breath, would have felt it catch in his throat.

Taking a step backward, he tried to hide in the shadows from Anna who might spot his pained expression. He didn't want to give any hint about his feelings for Marilla.

"My name is Marilla. How can I help you?" the shopkeeper asked, smiling at Anna.

"Uhm, yes," Anna said, glancing over her shoulder for some semblance of help from Harlem. As far as she could tell, he'd wandered off again.

Pursing her lips angrily, she looked back at the woman. "Yes, I actually have a friend who said you could help me."

"And a good friend at that," Marilla said with a smile. "I will do my best to help you out. What are you looking for?"

"Oh, I'm not necessarily looking for anything. I was hoping you could help me with a little," she hesitated, unsure of how to phrase it, "folklore information?"

The shop keeper's smile twitched slightly, showing that she wasn't pleased to not be making a sale.

Harlem had to chuckle quietly to himself. Marilla was still the same person as she ever was, a businesswoman.

Anna, not wanting to be here any longer than she had to, dug her phone out of her purse and opened the photo gallery. She held the screen face out toward Marilla. "Do you know what this is?" she asked, not wanting to give away too many details about the murder yet.

Leaning in and squinting, the woman's eyes rested on the image. She was silent a moment, no sign of recognition written on her expression. Then, as if something had hit her like a freight train, her eyes widened to the size of dinner plates. "Where did you find this?" she demanded, grabbing the phone out of Anna's hand and looking closer.

"Uh, up near Sunken Grove?"

"You just found it in a pool of water like this?" she asked, gasping.

"Well, sort of, yeah. Actually, my sister took these pictures and sent them to my phone."

Marilla shoved the phone back into Anna's hand. "Where is the dagger now? Please tell me you have it with you," she begged.

Anna nervously licked her lips, giving a sideways glance back to Harlem who was still standing off in the corner. This time, she spotted him standing there and realized he hadn't just wandered off. He only shook his head.

"We don't have it, as far as I know."

"Y-You just left it there?" she sputtered.

"No, we turned it over to the police because we didn't know *where* it had come from," she admitted, still skirting around the murder itself.

Marilla put a hand up to her forehead in distress. "You've got to be kidding me. Who sent you here? Who is this friend who said I'd know what this was?" she demanded.

Anna's mouth hung open. She didn't know how to answer that question. "U-Uh, they asked me not to say."

The woman cursed quietly. "Do you have any idea what that is?"

Anna, getting a little fed up, held out her arms. "No, of course, not. That's why I came to you."

Marilla folded her arms and scowled. "Its nickname is The Vampire Blade."

How fitting, Anna grumbled inwardly.

"It was one of many created by an ancient cannibal tribe who believed that by shedding the blood of your enemies you could gain their power and ability."

Anna couldn't help but grimace at the gross history lesson. Somehow, she felt even less sure that whoever had used the blade knew what it's original purpose was for.

"That is a dangerous tool to have around, even in a police station."

"Why? It's just a legend, isn't it?" Anna replied, playing the skeptic.

Marilla stepped close to her, their noses almost touching. "In the wrong hands, that blade could do some serious damage, and I don't mean just physically."

Taking a step back, Anna put space between herself and the shop owner. "Well, thanks for the help," she said, quickly turning to rush out of the building.

"I'm warning you. That blade has dark powers," she called out just before Anna was gone.

"What the heck? She's a nutball," Anna complained once she was back in the car.

"She's not a nutball," Harlem said defensively. "She just knows her relics, as well as their dark magical properties."

Anna shrugged. "So, what? Does that mean whoever killed Jason Dobbs also sucked up his lifeforce or something? What does that even mean, exactly?"

"I'm not sure, but if the killer really didn't know the knife had powers, they might be in for some surprises."

Before Anna could say anything else, her phone

began to vibrate. Picking it up, she realized it was her sister. "Hey, Belle. What's up?" she asked, answering the call.

"You won't believe what I found in the basement."

"You called me to talk about work? I need to get on the road back to Sunken Grove before it gets too late. I won't be getting back until seven-thirty or eight at this point."

"No, no, no. Listen to me," Belle insisted.

Anna could hear the excitement in her sister's voice and paused. "What? Did something happen?"

"In the basement. I found William Percy's dead body. Dan is having a look at things now."

"I'll be there as quick as I can," she said, hanging up the phone.

"Something wrong?" Harlem asked.

"We need to get back to Sunken Grove."

CHAPTER THIRTEEN

The drive-in parking lot was empty when Anna arrived. Full darkness had just fallen, which meant the movie should be playing. However, she had a good guess that Dan had requested they close for the evening, so he could continue his investigation.

However, she also didn't see Dan's police cruiser. Did that mean he had finished his investigation of the scene? Surely not.

Parking, she and Harlem rushed into the back door of the restaurant. "Belle?" she called out, stepping past the threshold.

"Right here," she said from where she sat at the counter.

"What happened? Where is Dan?" she asked,

walking over and tossing her purse on the counter before taking a seat next to her sister.

"He ran off to arrest Payton," she informed her.

"Arrest Payton?"

Belle nodded. "With William being dead, and Payton and William being the two main people connected to the murder weapon, he decided he needed to bring Payton in on suspicion of murder before he tried to skip town."

Anna sighed, clasping her hands on the countertop. She noticed her sister was drinking a beer and she instantly wished she had some wine. "I see. So, the original assumption was that William committed the crime and took off—which is why no one could find him. Now that he's dead, the assumption is that Payton killed both of them."

"That was what my thought was," Belle agreed. "He killed Jason for evicting him and then, after telling a lie about selling the dagger to William, he had to make sure William didn't blab the truth." Turning on the stool, she sipped her beer and looked Anna in the eye. "Speaking of the dagger, did you learn anything?"

"Only that it's a vampire dagger that steals power or something like that."

Belle's eyebrows shot up. "Woah. That's crazy."

"And I still don't see how it helps in our investigation," Anna pointed out.

"We just aren't seeing it yet, but I'm positive it ties in," Harlem noted.

Anna shook her head at him. "I'm not sure. I mean, what I want to know is *how* the body ended up in our basement. That seems like a more important detail at the moment. How could Payton get it down there without anyone noticing."

Belle shrugged. "I haven't the faintest idea. All I know is that the body *is* down there."

Anna's face went pale and she stood up. "You mean the body is still here?"

"Yeah, of course. Dan left the other officer here to keep an eye on the crime scene, and to keep anyone from going downstairs in the basement until he could secure Payton."

Just then, a loud male scream echoed through the kitchen.

"What was that?" Harlem asked.

In a flash, the girls were in a mad dash for the pantry where the trap door sat open. The police officer came bounding up the stairs, his face as white as a sheet.

"What happened? What's going on?"

"There's a huge bat down there. It flew right at me," he shouted, his voice squeaking. Clearly, this man did not do well with small rodents.

A tinkle of glass breaking echoed up from below.

"Uh-oh. Oh, no," Harlem gasped, floating through the trio of people standing at the entrance and heading down into the room below.

Without another hesitation, the girls pushed past the cop and followed the ghost down the steps.

"H-hey. You can't go down there. It's an official crime scene," the cop yelled, suddenly remembering his job again, but unwilling to go down and face the giant-sized bat again.

The sisters ignored him and ended up standing on the bottom landing. Looking around the room, they both saw that the window well had been broken out and the night air was whistling through.

"He's gone. He flew out the window," Harlem said.

The girls looked around. Belle instantly saw that the once full coffin was now very empty.

"Where did he go?" she asked.

"The dagger. The murder was committed right behind the movie screen," Harlem noted.

"So, what?" Belle asked, not seeing how any of this could possibly relate to a missing body or a bat attack.

"Don't you see?" Harlem demanded.

"The Vampire Dagger," Anna gasped in realization, looking at Harlem's black and white flickering figure and starting to come to a new hypothesis.

"What?" Belle demanded, still being on the outside of this latest deduction.

"Is it really possible? Could he have accidentally drawn out the powers of a vampire by killing someone behind the movie screen while the showing was going on?" Anna demanded, not even able to believe it herself.

"I think that's exactly what happened. He may not even have realized it until afterward."

"Wait, wait," Belle said, putting up a hand for silence so she could think. "Are you saying that William is the killer? He killed Jason while the movie was playing and because this dagger absorbs power, he somehow got turned into a vampire like the one in the film?"

"Exactly," Harlem said.

Belle let her jaw hang. "So, we've just unleashed a vampire on Sunken Grove."

"Seems so," Harlem gulped.

Anna licked her lips. "I think I might have an idea where he's heading. Come on."

CHAPTER FOURTEEN

Driving up outside of the old farmhouse, Anna leaped out of the driver seat as soon as the car was in park. Harlem quickly followed.

It had taken some convincing to make Belle stay behind, but they needed someone to tell the police officer what was going on and call Dan. Meanwhile, Anna hadn't hesitated to grab one important thing from among the props her sister had stored in the basement—something she had to ask Belle to pull out for her.

A cross.

It was made from plastic but painted to look like a gold relic from a Catholic church. She had it clutched tightly in her hand as she made her way up to the door of the house.

Unlike the movies, they didn't have things like holy water or sharpened stakes sitting around—and Anna highly doubted she would be staking anyone anyway, nor did she want to. The cross, however, was right there in the room with them where they'd discovered the body was missing.

She'd also grabbed a clove of garlic on her way through the kitchen and out the door.

She hoped she was prepared enough.

Opening the screen door of the porch, she began to hear the muffled cries from inside. "I think he's already in there," she shouted to Harlem, trying the doorknob. It didn't budge.

"Let me," Harlem insisted, floating through the door. Exerting some of his spiritual energy, he unlatched the deadbolt and let Anna through.

Once inside, Anna looked around to try and see where the mother and her children might be.

"Upstairs," Harlem said, pointing up the skinny front staircase to the second floor of the house.

"On it," she said, trotting up the steps and entering the first bedroom she saw. Stopping dead in the doorway, she saw the mother huddled in the corner. Standing over her with his back arched like a cat and his hands outstretched like claws was William Percy.

The kids weren't anywhere in sight and Anna was betting the mother had hidden them in another room.

"William!" Anna shouted, grabbing the monster's attention.

Spinning to look at the newcomer, he opened his mouth and hissed. Two needle-sharp fangs protruded from the top of his mouth. His eyes had a reddish glow that ran all the way through them and his nails appeared to have grown long and pointed.

Seemingly completely taken over by his new monstrous urges, he leaped at Anna.

In response, she lifted the cross in front of her.

The vampire shrieked in surprise, covering his face from the offending symbol.

"Now, Anna. Use the garlic," Harlem urged her.

"Right," she agreed, knowing this was her only chance. She had to act while he was distracted.

Digging the clove of garlic out of her pocket, she jumped forward and grabbed the vampire from behind, pushing the clove into his open mouth.

The sound that came out of him next was unlike anything she'd ever heard. It was like someone getting burned and crying out for help. The vampire slumped to the floor, coughing and sputtering until he lay still.

After a few moments of quiet, the mother stood up from her crouched position, still leaning on the wall. "Is he ... dead?"

"No, just knocked out, I think," Anna said.

The sound of the police car's sirens echoed in the distance. Dan was on his way.

"Better lay the cross on him now so he won't move or try to get away when he wakes up," Harlem suggested.

Agreeing, Anna did as he said and put it right on William's chest.

"A-Are you a vampire hunter?" the mother asked quietly.

Anna smiled, finding the comment humorous. "No, vampires don't exist," she said, wanting to convince her that William was, in fact, just a human who believed he was a vampire.

"I better go check on the kids," she said, running out of the room and down the hall.

"What's going on?" a man asked, stepping into the bedroom and seeing the strangers there, one of them knocked out on the floor. This was likely the father to the kids.

Before Anna could answer, Dan had come in the open front door and up the steps to handcuff the culprit.

CHAPTER FIFTEEN

"In today's morning news, William Percy, the suspected killer of Jason Dobbs, escaped the holding cell in Sunken Grove's police station sometime last night. Chief Bronson said that he still hasn't figured out how the suspect managed to get out of the cell, but that there was a strange pile of ashes on the floor this morning," a local radio announcer said as Belle and Anna worked in the kitchen to get things ready for that evening.

They were planning on picking up the marathon where they'd left off.

"You know what that means, don't you?" Harlem said, floating near the radio.

"What?" Anna asked, picking up a red and purple

frosted jelly filled donut from the nearby box. After the crazy night she'd had, doing something she never once in her life thought she'd do—hunting a vampire—she had decided that getting donuts and coffee from the local shop was a well-deserved treat.

Belle turned around from where she was organizing ingredients and took a sip of her chocolate hazelnut coffee her sister had purchased for her. "It means he was not in his coffin before the sun rose. Poof." She made an explosive motion with her free hand. "He turned to dust."

"That's what I assume, yes," Harlem agreed.

"I'm glad I convinced Dan to keep the cross near him for the rest of the night. I'm sure he thought I was crazy."

"Probably. I mean, I don't even think *he* believes in vampires."

"Neither do I," Anna insisted, biting into the sugary treat.

"How can you say that? You're probably the only living vampire hunter ever," Belle laughed.

Swallowing the bite and wiping a bit of raspberry

filling off her lip, Anna shook her head. "No, vampires don't exist. William Percy just happened to have some vampire-like qualities he'd absorbed from the movie."

"And he absorbed some of the weaknesses as well," Harlem pointed out, indicating that the cross and garlic had both worked.

"Thank goodness for that," Belle agreed, walking over to the box of donuts and selecting the traditional southern cruller. "Otherwise, how else would you have caught him? I mean, he would have either killed you or turned into a bat and flown away."

"Let's just concentrate on the fact that it didn't happen," Anna said. "Anyway, Diane got a bit of a spook."

"Diane?"

"She's the woman who lives in that house now."

"Ah, yes," Belle said.

"Thankfully, the kids were already asleep in bed when the bat came in. I guess William just wanted to reclaim his home any way he could."

"That's another thing. How did you know he would be going there?" Belle asked.

"When I talked to Diane yesterday, she mentioned thinking she saw a lurker outside. When I realized William was still alive . . . or as alive as a vampire can be, I thought it was him. I just deduced that he was heading back there again."

Belle beamed, munching on her cruller. "You know, I'm proud of you."

"Me?"

"Yeah, you took on this whole scary case almost single-handedly."

"No, I had help from both of you," Anna indicated, nodding to her sister and the ghost. "I'm just glad we got it all figured out before more damage could be done."

"Yeah. Just think, we could have had a vampire living in our basement for a while and we wouldn't have even known it."

"We would have found him eventually," Harlem said.

"Anyway, I'm just glad it's over and we *don't* have a vampire living in our basement," Anna admitted.

"Nope. Just on the movie screen again," Belle said.

"Honestly, I could do without another vampire movie for the rest of my life," Anna joked, taking a long drink of her dark roast coffee blend.

Belle and Harlem laughed out loud.

ALSO BY CAROLYN Q. HUNTER

Diner of the Dead Series

Book 1: The Wicked Waffle

Book 2: Battered and Buttered Waffle

Book 3: Sinister Strawberry Waffle

Book 4: The Wayward Waffle

Book 5: Pumpkin Pie Waffle

Book 6: Turkey and Terror

Book 7: Creepy Christmas Waffle

Book 8: Birthday Cake Waffle

Book 9: Spooky Sweetheart Waffle

Book 10: Eerie Irish Waffle

Book 11: Savory Spring Waffle

Book 12: Benedict Waffle

Book 13: Scary Sausage Waffle

Book 14: Murderous Mocha Waffle

Book 15: Red Velvet Waffle

Book 16: High Steaks Murder

Book 17: Hole In One Waffle

Book 18: Fireworks and Waffles

Book 19: Games, Ghouls and Waffles

Book 20: Waffling in Murder

The Wicked Waffle Series

Book 1: Hot Buttered Murder

Book 2: Bacon Caramel Murder

Book 3: Thanksgiving Waffle Murder

Book 4: Christmas Waffle Caper

Book 5: Buckaroo Waffle Murder

Book 6: Wedding Waffle Murder

Book 7: Cactus Waffle Murder

Book 8: Zombie Waffle Murder

Book 9: A Very Catty Murder

Book 10: Halloween Waffle Murder

Pies and Pages Series

Book 1: Killer Apple Pie

Book 2: Killer Chocolate Pie

Book 3: Killer Halloween Pie

Book 4: Killer Thanksgiving Pie

Book 5: Killer Christmas Pie

Book 6: Killer Caramel Pie

Book 7: Killer Cocoa Pie

Book 8: Shamrock Pie Murder

Book 9: Killer Easter Pie

Book 10: Killer Cheesecake Tart

Book 11: Summer Smore Murder

Book 12: Maple Nut Murder

Book 13: Tea, Thyme, and Murder

Book 14: A Harvest of Murder

Book 15: Perfectly Pumpkin Killer

Book 16: Killer Acorn Pie

Book 17: Killer Chocolate Pecan Pie

Dead-End Drive-In Series

Book 1: Sisterly Screams

Book 2: Moans, Mummies and Murder

Book 3: Blue Eyed Doll

Book 4: Movies and Murder

The Cracked Mirror Series

Book 1: The Biker and The Boogeyman

AUTHOR'S NOTE

I'd love to hear your thoughts on my books, the storylines, and anything else that you'd like to comment on—reader feedback is very important to me. My contact information, along with some other helpful links, is listed below. If you'd like to be on my list of "folks to contact" with updates, release and sales notifications, etc.... just shoot me an email and let me know. Thanks for reading!

Also...

... if you're looking for more great reads, I am proud to announce that Summer Prescott Books publishes several popular series by Cozy authors Gretchen Allen and Patti Benning, as well as Carolyn Q. Hunter, Blair Merrin, Susie Gayle and more!

CONTACT SUMMER PRESCOTT BOOKS PUBLISHING

Twitter: @summerprescott1

Blog and Book Catalog: http://summerprescottbooks.com

Email: summer.prescott.cozies@gmail.com

And...look up The Summer Prescott Fan Page and Summer Prescott Publishing Page on Facebook – let's be friends!

To download a free book, and sign up for our fun and exciting newsletter, which will give you opportunities to win prizes and swag, enter contests, and be the first to know about New Releases, click here: http://summerprescottbooks.com